Print information available on the last page

Rev. date: 10/12/2018

To order additional copies of this book, contact:
Xlibris
1-888-795-4274
www.Xlibris.com
Orders@Xlibris.com

DEDICATION

If God gave me the opportunity to
choose a family, I would choose mine.

To my sons, John, Ken, Gary, Michael
Dan and my very special daughter
AnnMarie. Thank you for always being
there with your encouragement and help.

Thank you

To my niece Diane Hynes DelDuca for your
expertise and guidance in this book and
my friend Susan Berger thank you again
for your beautiful illustrations.

The trees are sleeping...

It's very cold out today and as I look

out the window – I see trees

I see trees with no leaves

I see trees with empty birds nests.

It is winter here now and the birds have left us to go to warmer places.

The leaves in October turned from green
to red, yellow, orange and purple.

The leaves in November start falling
off the trees, they sometimes even look
like colorful snowflakes as they fall...

We pile them up, we play in them
and we try to catch them...

We bring them to school,
we trace and color them
to make Thanksgiving decorations.

Now the leaves are all gone and the trees
have gone to sleep.

We can see through
them and see more of the blue sky.

We wait for the long cold winter to end,
then we see little green buds forming
on the bare branches.

We wait, we watch, the weather
gets warmer and the sun makes the
trees wake up.

The brand new baby leaves fill our trees.
When they grow up they give us shade
from the summer sun.

As we enjoy our picnics, bar-be-cues,
baseball games and long walks in the
park – green trees send us - cool breezes
and shade - to protect us from the hot
summer sun.

We have no school and
have so much fun. And then ----

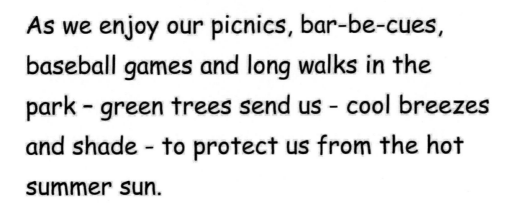

We wait, we watch and the weather
gets colder and colder...

Can you guess what happens?

The leaves start to change color...

The leaves start to fall...

The weather gets colder.

And the trees go back to sleep.

Printed in the United States
by Baker & Taylor Publisher Services